Paul Ro

A Christmas Without Santa

Bumblebee Books
London

A CIP catalogue record for this title is
available from the British Library.

ISBN: 978-1-83934-321-6

Bumblebee Books is an imprint of
Olympia Publishers.

First Published in 2022

Bumblebee Books
Tallis House
2 Tallis Street
London
EC4Y 0AB

Printed in Great Britain

www.olympiapublishers.com

Dedication

I dedicate this book to my wife and three children, Charlie, Emily and Maisie, who we have shared many wonderful Christmases together. Thank you for always being there for me and supporting me.

Chapter 1
No Show

"Slow Dasher, Slow Blitzen," called out Santa. They had finally arrived back at the North Pole after delivering presents to the children of the world. Santa was glad to be back home. He loved delivering the presents and eating all the mince pies and cookies, but it was a really tiring night for him. He was looking forward to getting into his big, warm, cosy bed. He was already starting to think about what he would dream about, the same thing he dreamed about every night: Christmas.

The snow was falling heavily now, in the North Pole. It was going to be another white Christmas. It would be the six-hundredth Christmas that it had snowed at the North Pole. Well, that's what Santa thought, as he could no longer remember the exact number of white Christmases. It could've been more, it could've been less, but all the years now seemed the same to him.

"Another white Christmas again this year," Santa called out to Blitzen. Blitzen nodded in agreement, with a reindeer smile on his snowy face. Santa said the same thing every year. The reindeers knew what he was going to say but they never got fed up of hearing it when he did say it. The reindeers just loved it; it wouldn't have been the same if he didn't. It's just like when a dad tells his dad-jokes at Christmas. The children know their dad is going to do it but they just roll their eyes with embarrassment and shake their heads, thinking him silly but, really, deep down, loving it when he does. The reindeers were just the same with Santa.

Without Santa, there would be no Christmas and, without Christmas, the reindeers wouldn't have the magic to make themselves fly through the night sky. Without the reindeers, the elves wouldn't be able to put all the presents they make for Santa to deliver to all the boys and girls of the world every Christmas on the sleigh for them to pull. Without Santa, Christmas would not exist – but that would never happen. Could it …? Would it …? No, that would never happen. There would always be Santa, so there would always be Christmas.

Santa pulled on the reins and steered the sleigh right into the large reindeer stable. The elves were there ready and waiting for them to return. They loved it when Santa returned on Christmas morning because they knew it was now only 364 days to the next Christmas Eve sleigh ride. They could start planning, building and preparing all over again; it would be one day closer to Christmas Eve. The elves were clapping and cheering with excitement. They all started to sing 'Jingle Bells' as Santa landed. This was their favourite song. The sleigh and the reindeer landed gently and smoothly in the stable. Santa took off his hat and he flung it towards a hat stand, where it landed perfectly on the hook, the one that had Santa's name and picture on it. "Wow, what another great night that was. Thank-you so much, boys and girls. It was a pleasure riding with you again tonight. You have done exceptionally well and you have again deserved a good rest."

The reindeers were taken by the elves to their own paddock in the stable. As soon as the reindeers had settled down in their nice, warm, cosy straw bed, they were fast asleep. You could even hear one of the reindeers snoring. The elves were not sure who this was but it might have been Cupid.

Santa leaped out of his sleigh. He hung up his coat next to his hat, took off his snowy wellies, and left the stable. The elves followed, closing the door behind them, making sure they were quiet. They didn't want to wake the reindeers; they needed their rest and sleep. Well, have you ever seen a grumpy reindeer? No. Well, you don't want to!

Santa headed straight into his living room where Mrs Claus was waiting for him with a big mug of hot chocolate. The hot chocolate was as big as ever and filled with whipped cream, marshmallows, chocolate shavings and just a hint of caramel sauce. Santa looked forward to this the most. Even when he was in the coldest towns, villages and cities, he knew that the hot chocolate would warm him up when he returned home. He had drunk warm milk, cold milk, sherry and other drinks that had been left for him by all the boys and girls, but nothing could beat Mrs Claus's hot chocolate. It was delicious.

"Good night tonight?" asked Mrs Claus.

Santa sat down in his big, comfy chair. He looked at Mrs Claus and repeated what he said to her every year, "The best." Santa sat in his chair and drank his hot chocolate all in one go, leaving bits of chocolate and a marshmallow in his beard. Santa wiped his beard with a tissue, wiping the chocolate away. He then picked the marshmallow out of his beard and put it in his mouth and ate it. "Time for me to go to bed I think, Mrs Claus. It's been a long exhausting night," said Santa.

"I think you are right," said Mrs Claus.

Santa made his way to his bedroom feeling very happy with himself that he was making so many children of the world happy. He was looking forward to a good sleep. But, he was more looking forward to waking up and getting to read the letters from the children. He was really looking forward to hearing from the children through the letters they would send to him, thanking him for all their presents and for everything that he, the reindeers and the elves had done for them. This is what made Santa's Christmas. He was imagining how much joy the presents had brought to them; it brought a lot of joy to him to know that he had made the children happy. Just thinking about the smiles on their faces brought a big grin to Santa's face. He sometimes wished that he could be there to see the children open their presents but he knew that the second-best part of being Santa would be getting the thank-you letters from the children. He loved opening and reading all the letters from them and the Christmas joy it brought to him was the best feeling in the world.

Santa started getting dressed to get into bed. He put on his favourite pyjamas, the same pyjamas he always wore after delivering his presents – his reindeer ones. While getting ready, Santa started singing his favourite Christmas song, 'Santa Claus has been to town.' "I've made a list. I've checked it twice. I already know who's been naughty and nice. I have been to town. I have been to town." Santa climbed into bed and was now ready to settle down and enjoy his sleep. Santa had done his part now, and he knew he had the best part of Christmas – delivering the presents. He knew he had the best job in the world and he wouldn't or couldn't want to do any other job. Why would he?

Thirty-six hours later, Santa arose out of his bed. He was refreshed and ready to meet up with the elves and start working on preparing for next Christmas. He only had 363 days left to be ready. It was Christmas every day at the North Pole. Who wouldn't love to celebrate Christmas every day? Santa, Mrs Claus and the elves loved it. It was always white with snow outside. The Christmas spirit was alive at the North Pole and it was the most fantastic and most beautiful place in the world. Santa made his way to the living room where Mrs Claus was waiting at the table for him. "Good morning. How are you feeling this morning?"

"I feel well rested now, and I'm looking forward to opening and seeing all the thank-you letters that have come since I've been asleep." Mrs Claus looked away sheepishly and didn't answer him. She didn't know what to say. She was unsure what to do. How could she tell him? What would she tell him? How was he going to react? Mrs Claus carried on preparing Santa's breakfast and tried to change the subject.

"Well, Mr Claus, shall we take a nice walk around the pole this morning and see if we can see any whales? Or Polar bears playing? Or shall we just have a walk?"

"No. I think I will eat my breakfast and start reading the letters," said Santa.

"OK," said Mrs Claus, quietly.

Santa started his breakfast. He had bacon, sausages, black pudding, mushrooms, toast and his favourite hot chocolate drink. Santa always ate his breakfast after his long sleep really quickly. Even before Mrs Claus had finished washing up, it was all gone. Santa was super excited to open the letters that were awaiting him. He would have opened the letters first, but his tummy was rumbling away. It needed food. Santa quickly ate all his breakfast in record time this year. "That certainly filled a gap in my tummy, Mrs Claus. Now, it's time to go and sort those letters out," said Santa.

"Hang on a moment. Maybe you should leave it for a couple of days and relax. You've had a busy Christmas and the letters will still be there in a couple of days after you have rested. You need your rest," said Mrs Claus.

"No. You know I love reading the letters as soon as I get up from my sleep and it's a tradition that I read the letters. The Christmas spirit and the happiness the gifts have brought the children is what I love reading about. Those letters are what makes me look forward to Christmas Eve next year. The joy it brings to them is what my Christmas is all about," said Santa.

Santa made his way to the chimney delivery room. This is the room where all the letters to the North Pole come. Sent by the children, they would come down this chimney and reach Santa. Santa would be in there for days, going through the children's letters and, sometimes, there would be a couple of adult letters in there, too. Santa was in a hurry, nearly breaking into a run to get there more quickly than ever before. Behind him, Mrs Claus was following more slowly and gingerly than Santa. She didn't know what she was going to do when Santa found out. She didn't know what to say. There was nothing she could say. Santa was going to find out soon enough.

Santa opened the two big doors of the chimney room. As he opened the door, he was smiling from ear to ear. The excitement he had was a warm, fuzzy feeling running through him. This is what Santa felt every year and he believed this is how the children felt on Christmas morning when they saw all the presents that he had left for them. This was Santa's Christmas morning.

As Santa entered the room, he looked around. He could not believe what he was seeing. Santa stood there, open mouthed, for what seemed like an eternity. "What is this? What is going on? Could this be really happening?" Santa said, softly.

He would soon find out.

Chapter 2
Open To Offers

Santa took a couple of steps forward into the room. He did three full circles, looking around and surveying what was in front of him. To his amazement, there was NOTHING there, nothing to be seen, just an open fireplace and his own reading chair. The room should've been full of letters, full of paper, just … full. But there was nothing, not even a scrap of paper, not one single envelope, not one postage stamp. Nothing. Mrs Claus finally entered the room with her head down low, not saying a word.

"What's this, Mrs Claus? What's happening? Where are the letters? What …? Where …? How …? Where are the letters?" Santa said, with fear in his voice. He had so many emotions going through him at this point that he felt sick. He felt – well, he didn't quite know how he felt, but he didn't like the way he was feeling.

"There must be a blockage in the chimney. I will get Chimney, the elf…" (Yes, that was his name. No – not elf – Chimney) "…to take a look and remove any blockages up there. We can come back tomorrow and you can start reading all the letters. Everything will be ready and back to normal for you, you'll see," said Mrs Claus.

"Yes, that's a good idea. I must have so many letters

coming this year that the letters have blocked the chimney so they can't come down. I think I may have a quick look now, myself, and sort it out," said Santa, with a bit more enthusiasm in his voice.

"No!" yelled Mrs Claus. "You can't do that." She desperately tried to think of something to say. "Urm... urm... urm... You may get all messy from the dirt and soot—and, and, and—you have got your best 'letter-reading-clothes' on. You wouldn't want them to get dirty and then all the letters will get dirty when you are reading them. Let's leave it to Chimney, the elf," said Mrs Claus, with concern and anxiety in her voice.

Santa agreed and nodded as he and Mrs Claus left the chimney reading room, closing the doors behind him. Mrs Claus was hoping that this was true. Surely, the letters had to be somewhere. They had to be there. Mrs Claus crossed her fingers, hoping that this would be fixed and that it was the issue. There could be no other explanation.

As Santa and Mrs Claus entered the living room, Santa had not said a single word since he had left the chimney room. He just walked, shaking his head and muttering to himself, "Why is there nothing there? Where are my letters?"

Santa sat down in his chair with a puzzled look on his face. He had never felt like this before. This feeling was unknown to him. He didn't like it. He didn't want to feel this way. This should have been his favourite time of the day and, probably, the second-best part of the year but here he was – doing nothing.

"Don't worry, Mr Claus, this will be all sorted by tomorrow and you can get on with reading the letters tomorrow. You can forget about the problems we have had today," said Mrs Claus.

"Yes, you are right, Mrs Claus. It's just so strange that

there are no letters. I haven't known us to have any problems here at the North Pole before with this issue. Or, come to think of it, to have any issues with anything. Maybe it's what they call the 'Christmas gremlins'. Maybe, we were due one," said Santa, with a bit of laughter in his voice.

Santa decided to relax in his chair for the rest of the day. He tried not to think about not having any letters but it just kept playing on his mind. Why was the room empty? Where were the letters? What had happened? Nothing like this had ever happened before. Santa sat there worrying. His mind was going over and over with questions. After a while, he started to relax and he finally fell asleep in his chair.

Mrs Claus decided that she would leave him there for the night, so she covered him with a blanket and kissed him on his forehead. "Goodnight, Mr Claus. This will all be sorted in the morning and we will be back to normal. I hope…" she whispered. Mrs Claus hoped she was right. She really did. She didn't like Santa feeling this way but there was nothing she could do about it. All she could do was to wish for a Christmas miracle.

The morning finally came and Santa woke up even earlier than usual. He showered, got dressed and made his way to the kitchen. He was in so much of a hurry that he skipped breakfast. He had never done this before but he just wanted to get reading; he was already a day behind. He was almost jogging to get to the chimney room – not a slow walk, not a brisk walk but a full jog. The elves in the hallway could not believe what they were seeing. Santa was jogging. The elves started muttering to each other, looking quite shocked and surprised at what they were witnessing. Some of the elves had a look of shock, some had smiles on their faces – and then, there was Chimney. He didn't have any emotions showing or going through him, just nothing. He was as white as the snow that lay outside. He felt sick and he knew Santa would feel the same way shortly. Santa got to the doors of the chimney room. He flung them open and, again, he was amazed. Santa stopped. He was paralysed, rooted to the spot, not able to move, not able to say a word. He just stood there, again, looking in the room for something – anything. But, again, there was nothing there. Santa was closely followed by Mrs Claus and Chimney into the room. They both just stood there waiting for Santa to say something – anything – but Santa was speechless.

After what seemed to be a lifetime, Santa finally spoke. "What's the issue Chimney? Why are there no letters coming down the chimney? Could you not fix the blockage? What do I need to do to help you? What…? Tell me! Show me! Explain to me. Tell me something – anything …" said Santa, with a tear in his eye. Mrs Claus looked at Chimney. Chimney looked at Santa. Santa looked at both of them. "What is happening?" asked Santa.

Chimney walked towards the fireplace and jumped onto the opening of the fire grate where he explained to Santa that there was no blockage in the chimney. The chimney was as it had always been, clean, spotless and ready to receive any letters that had been sent. He could not explain to Santa why the letters had not come and why the room was empty. He didn't like telling Santa this but he could not lie to him. He had to tell the truth. Elves always told the truth and they could never lie. This was the hardest thing that any elf had ever had to tell Santa. Chimney was tearful and upset because he could not help Santa and he was soon struggling to put a sentence together. He just kept saying, "Sorry." Santa walked over to the chimney to look for himself and, to his dismay, as he looked up the chimney, he could see that there was no blockage, no letters, no nothing.

"What was going on?" he thought. "There is no need to apologise, Chimney, it's not your fault. I just can't explain what is going on," he said. Santa wandered around the room trying to think of the answer to what was going on but he had more questions than he had answers. Fingers on his chin, rubbing his beard, trying to think, trying to come up with an explanation, trying to find a logical reason to why there were no letters, but Santa could not come up with any. He slumped in his chair and sat there thinking, thinking about what he was going to do.

There was silence in the room for over a minute when Mrs Claus came over to him and said, "It's OK dear. Maybe the children are enjoying all the gifts that you have delivered to them and they haven't got round to writing to you yet. You know how busy the children and the adults of the world are today. There is so much going on in their lives and I'm sure, in the next couple of days, the letters will start to come and we will look back at this and laugh about being worried about nothing."

"Yes. You are right, Mrs Claus," said Santa, with a bit of enthusiasm in his voice as he leaped out of his chair, "I'm going to the stables to check on the reindeers." Mrs Claus was really hoping that this was going to be the case and that everything would be fine. She had never seen Santa like this before. She missed the jolly old Mr Claus she had become accustomed to.

The next couple of mornings Santa got up and did the same thing. He went straight to the chimney room looking for the letters. But, as the days went on, he looked more and more disappointed every morning. There were no letters, no nothing. The Christmas spirit was leaving him more and more by the day. He felt sad. It was starting to affect not just Santa, but also Mrs Claus, the elves and even the reindeers. They were not just sad because there were no letters. They were sad because Santa was sad. What was going on with the letters? Why were they not coming? Why…? Why…? Why…? That is all everyone kept asking at the North Pole. Why were there no letters? Why had the children not written? Why? I don't know why – but why?

Santa was at a loose end. He didn't know what to do. Nobody knew what to do. This had never happened before. This was new to everybody. Did Santa forget to deliver the presents and that's why no children had written to him? No. Santa had definitely delivered the presents. He would never forget to do that!

It was now New Year's Eve and it was the big North Pole New Year's Eve party. Nobody was in the mood for a party but the elves thought that, if they had a good time, enjoyed the food, the games and the dancing, then, maybe, in the New Year, the letters would start to come and things would be back to normal with just a slight delay. The night started slowly with everyone staying in their chairs looking sad and a little depressed. There was no singing, no dancing and no one was wanting to have a good time. Having a good time was the last thing on everyone's mind.

Mrs Claus finally got up on the dance floor and she started to dance by herself. Then, she was joined by Chimney. Then, another elf joined in. Then another. Then, all of the elves were dancing on the dance floor, dancing to their favourite songs.

There was 'Dance like an elf', 'Twist and boogie like elf', 'Elf music man' and everyone's favourite, 'Who let Santa out?' This made Santa get up and dance. This always made Santa dance, no matter where or what he was doing. This was Santa's song. He sang and danced like no one better. This was his song. The night went by quickly and, before anyone realised, it was eight seconds to the New Year: 8, 7, 6, 5, 4, 3, 2, 1 …

"Happy New year everyone!" called out Santa.

Everyone cheered and then everyone joined in with the elf New Year song:

"Another year has gone by and we have cheered,
The big man is done now he's all delivered.
We, the elves, make the toys all year,
We never have to make a chandelier.
Santa Claus, the reindeer, have been through the sky,
The children never seem to ask, 'why?'
We can't wait to start work again real soon,
Christmas is the best; it's like dancing on the moon.
A New Year has come in,
For us it's a win, win.
Happy New Year from me to you,
Our parties are the best, and that is true.
So, Happy New Year to you, one and all,
Now, let's all dance like the snowfall."

When the party had finished, Santa decided to go and have a look at the chimney room, hoping that the letters had started to arrive. He and Mrs Claus walked down the corridor still humming the elf New Year song. They opened the door to the chimney room and to their surprise it had finally happened. For the first time ever, Santa had not received one single thank-you letter before the New Year had come in. "Don't worry," said

Mrs Claus. "We will come and have a look in the morning, after we have been to sleep, and then, hopefully, the letters will be here for you."

"Yes. You are probably right, Mrs Claus, it's been a long day. Let's get to sleep now," said Santa.

Santa got into bed but he just couldn't drop off or get to sleep. There were so many things going around his head. He was wondering what he was going to do and what had happened to the letters. Santa didn't sleep a wink all night. He tossed, he turned, he fidgeted; he just couldn't settle. He finally decided what he was going to do. He would check the chimney room one more time when he got up and, if there were no letters, he had decided what he was going to do. He could no longer wait for the letters so he had made his decision. His decision was now set in place. Santa's decision was going to be final. No one could change his mind or convince him to do anything differently.

Santa finally dropped off to sleep and woke up a couple of hours later. When he woke up, he found himself in the bed all alone. He got up, dressed and went to the kitchen. He was expecting to see Mrs Claus in there but she was not there. He then checked the living room and then the stables but she couldn't be found. He made his way to the chimney room. As he was approaching, Santa could see that the door was open. There was lots of noise coming from inside, lots of different voices. He couldn't quite hear what was being said. He could hear Chimney, Mrs Claus and a few of the other elves' voices but he couldn't quite make out the conversation. Santa entered the room and, when he did, the room fell silent. You could hear a pin drop. You could hear the mice squeak. You could even hear the wings of the fly buzzing around the room. Not one single word was spoken, not a noise was made – nothing. There was complete silence. Santa looked around and a tear started to fall from his eye, running down his red, rosy cheek.

Santa fell to his knees on the floor, with his hands on his head, shaking his head with disappointment. Mrs Claus knelt down next to him and said, "I'm sure they will come in in a day or two. We just need to be patient." She placed her arm around him for comfort and whispered, "It will be OK. Let's just go and have a few days' rest and then assess the situation later on."

At this point, Santa stood up and looked at everyone in the room. They all looked back at him. Many of the elves already had tears in their eyes. Some of the elves were just standing there in silence, doing and saying nothing, just waiting for Santa to speak. Santa cleared his throat and, with a whisper and looking at the floor, quietly said, "This is it. This is it. It is now time." He looked at the elves. He wiped his tears away from his face and said to them all, with a soft tone, and with no hesitation in his voice. He spoke clearly, "Today, elves, I have decided that I will no longer be Santa Claus and I will not be delivering presents again to the children of the world."

The elves and Mrs Claus were in shock. Some of the elves fainted and passed out. Some just stood there, and then some of the elves just laughed because they didn't know what to do. They thought Santa was joking. But Santa was not joking. He had made his decision and he was going to stick to this decision.

Chapter 3
Starting Again

"What did you say, Mr Claus, did I just hear you right? I think I just misheard what you said?" said Mrs Claus. Santa looked at Mrs Claus with no emotions in his face, no tears, no smile, no nothing – just looking at her face to face.

Santa spoke softly and clearly. "Mrs Claus, you did hear me correctly. The time has now come for me to no longer be Santa Claus. The children of the world no longer need or appreciate us here at the North Pole, and I feel that the children no longer have the Christmas spirit within them. They don't appreciate the effort, the time and the sacrifices that we make for them." The elves looked in disbelief at what was being said to them. What had they had just heard? It couldn't be right. Santa would never give up being Santa Claus. He loved being Santa. He was loved by everyone. The elves started to think that it was just a big joke – but it wasn't April Fool's Day. It was New Year's Day.

Santa, again, looked at everyone in the room and everyone, again, stood there in silence waiting for Santa to speak. "Yes, you have heard me right and you have heard me well in what I have just announced to you. It is with a heavy heart that I, Santa, will not be getting in the sleigh with the reindeers again on Christmas Eve. I will not be delivering all the presents that you the elves have made and I will not be jingling any more bells in a one-horse open sleigh. I have thought very hard and long about my decision and I now believe the children of the world have spoken. They no longer need, want, or believe in me, so now is the time for me to start something new. We have had many good years and centuries of fulfilling the wishes and dreams of the children and, without you, all the Christmases, in which we helped to make their dreams and wishes come true, wouldn't have been possible," said Santa.

The elves started shouting out all at once. "You can't go Santa! We need you! The children really need and believe in you! This is just a one off! The letters will come!"

Santa looked at Mrs Claus and Mrs Claus looked at Santa. She knew by just looking at him and, without him saying another word, she knew that he had made his choice. She knew that this was the end of Santa. Mrs Claus spoke softly and precisely and asked Santa. "Is this what you truly want to do? You no longer want to be Santa?"

Santa thought for a moment. He thought about all the letters he had received through the years, all the cookies he had eaten, all the sights he had seen when riding in his sleigh and all the good times that he had had. But he knew that, over the last couple of years, he had noticed a change. He had known, deep down, that this time would come. The Christmas magic was slowly fading away. There were fewer and fewer thank-you letters coming to the North Pole. The children didn't seem to believe in him as much now. So, Santa did not see the point of him carrying on being Santa if the Christmas belief was not there.

Santa took Mrs Claus's hands and held them tight. Looking her in eyes, he spoke with love and affection in his voice. "Yes, Mrs Claus, this is what we need to do. We have done this for so long and I am forever grateful for all the joy being Santa has brought me. I have enjoyed and loved every minute and having you by my side is everything that I could have ever have needed or wanted. So, yes. This is the end, the end of me being Santa."

Santa and Mrs Claus started to cry. The elves gathered around them and they started a massive hug in the middle of the room. Everyone was crying. Everyone was upset.

The following morning, Santa and Mrs Claus sat in the kitchen, thinking about the previous day and the decision that they had chosen to make. It felt really strange to both of them but, now, they had to start thinking about their new beginnings.

The elves were also thinking about things and the questions that they needed answering. A new beginning, a new adventure for Santa and Mrs Claus but – what could they do? Where would they go? What would happen to the elves? What would happen to the North Pole? The reindeers? Would they ever fly again? So many questions that the elves didn't think that they would ever have to ask Santa or themselves, but they did need to ask them. They desperately had to find the answers to the questions because Santa was to be no more!

The elves tried desperately to convince Santa to stay. They tried everything. They pleaded, they begged him, they cried with him and they even hung on to him but Santa just kept saying the same thing. "It's over. There will be no more Santa."

Santa and Mrs Claus sat in the kitchen. They needed to decide where to go, when to go and what they would do when they did go. Neither one had ever thought that they would have to leave the North Pole. They never thought they could leave it behind. Santa and Mrs Claus decided to call out places that they could go and try to narrow it down, hopefully finding the right place for both of them. They started calling out place names.

"Dubai," said Mrs Claus.

"No, that is way too hot for me, Mrs Claus. I think we would both struggle there and I don't think I'd like the sand that much," said Santa.

"Australia," said Santa.

"Urm, urm … No way!" yelled out Mrs Claus. They have spiders, snakes – some dangerous – and poisonous spiders and snakes. I couldn't live there. Spiders are everywhere and snakes wrap themselves around rakes. So – no way!"

"The Amazon rainforest," said Mrs Claus. Santa looked puzzled and he tried to keep a straight face about what Mrs Claus had just said to him but he could not hold it in. He erupted with laughter.

"If you think Australia is bad, my sweet, then the Amazon rainforest is so much worse – a lot worse. There are not just spiders and snakes to worry about. They have jaguars, piranhas, giant centipedes and more than I can think of at this time, Mrs Claus."

"Oh! Silly me," said Mrs Claus, who was now laughing. "I just wasn't thinking." The laughter lifted their spirits. They realised that this was going to be so hard for both of them, but it was never going to be an easy decision to make. The North Pole is a one-in-a-million-place, the best place on earth, so finding somewhere else was not going to be an easy task. Throughout the day, they started thinking and calling out countries, cities, towns – anywhere they could go – just trying to come up with ideas, suggestions and places that they could think of.

"China!"

"Too many people."

"South pole!"

"Not enough people."

"Japan!"

"We don't like raw fish."

"Mexico!"

"Food is way too spicy."

"Space!"

"No oxygen."

"Under the sea!"

"Now we are getting silly."

Santa and Mrs Claus could not come up with any suitable ideas or agree on where to go. They could not agree on anything. Santa then came up with an idea. He walked over to the globe that he had on his bookcase. He decided that he would get the globe. He would then spin the globe and, while it was spinning, Mrs Claus would stop it with her finger and that would be the place they would go. Santa picked up the globe and he began to spin the globe. "Whenever you are ready, Mrs Claus, just stop the globe."

Mrs Claus said, "After three I will stop it. One…, Two…, Three…" Mrs Claus stopped the globe. She lifted her finger and they both looked at where they would be moving to, their new home. They couldn't believe it. They couldn't go there. Out of all the places in the world, she had put her finger on probably the one place where they could never go: the Bermuda Triangle.

"I think we will try that again, Mrs Claus. First go is always a practice," chuckled Santa.

Santa began to spin the globe once again: "One..., Two..., Three..." called out Mrs Claus. She stopped the globe. Again, Mrs Claus lifted her finger and looked at the globe to find out where their new home would be.

They both looked at each other and both called out, "Skye, Scotland."

This was a fun game. But, then Mrs Claus realised it wasn't a game. This was happening. This was going to be their life from now on. She had to get ready to leave the North Pole. She had forgotten for a short moment that she was about to leave her home, her friends, the elves and the place she loved. She had to – and she wanted to follow Santa. She loved him. She knew his heart was no longer in it to be Santa any more. His decision had been made and she respected his decision. The disappointment of receiving no letters after Christmas was too much for him. She had seen a decline in the letters being sent over the last couple of years but she had never thought it would get to the point where none came. She had hoped that things would improve but, sadly, it hadn't.

Santa and Mrs Claus agreed that they would start their new life tomorrow. They didn't want to wait. It would be harder leaving the North Pole if they stayed any longer than necessary. They would pack everything that they needed and set off to Skye. But, first, they had to get the elves and the reindeers together. Santa would tell them what was happening and he would tell them all where Santa and Mrs Claus's new home was going to be.

So, now that they knew where their new life was going to take them, they gathered all the elves and reindeers outside the stable and they both started to tell all of them where they were going to go. "Thank-you for everything that you have done for us both over the years. Thank you for making all the presents for every boy and girl. Without you, no child would've been able to enjoy Christmas and I ..., and I ..." Santa started to stutter. The realisation of what he was saying had hit him. Santa took a big deep breath, trying to compose himself. "I would not have been able to have been Santa for so long if it wasn't for everything that you do and have done. We have known each other for more centuries than I can remember and I will miss every one of you. You will always hold a special place in my heart, everyone one of you. You are like sons and daughters to me and Mrs Claus and I wish that we could continue to carry on with the Santa tradition at Christmas. But the children of the world no longer need me. The Christmas magic will remain in every one of you and the reindeers but, as soon as me and Mrs Claus leave the North Pole without a reindeer or an elf, our Christmas magic will be gone. We will not be able to return. I will still believe in you all. I wish you all the luck for the future and I will never forget you. Our new home will be in Skye, Scotland," said Santa, with tears now falling down his face.

The elves were really upset now, and there were lots of tears. Some of the elves were fainting. The stables were an unhappy place. I'm even sure that the reindeers were crying, but I'm not certain of this because I've never seen a reindeer cry.

"We will be leaving the North Pole in the morning. We will take the sleigh with us and Cupid and Comet will take us to our new home in Scotland. When we reach Scotland, I will then send them back to the North Pole," explained Santa to the elves.

A decision had now been made. They had a plan. They

knew when they would be going and where their new home would be. They had even decided on how they would get to Skye. Santa was excited about his new life, his new adventure. But, deep down, he knew that he would miss being Santa. It would be strange for him and Mrs Claus. This, their new life, was their fresh start.

Chapter 4
Anguish For The Elves?

The following morning, Santa and Mrs Claus put everything that they were going to need on the sleigh. The sleigh was packed with all the clothes, photos and many more items that they had collected over the centuries. For some reason, I think it may have been for sentimental reasons, Santa took his santa suit with him. Well – he was actually wearing it. Santa and Mrs Claus stepped into the sleigh. They both sat down and they started to wave to the elves as they got ready to get going.

Santa called out, "On Comet! On Cupid! Off we go to Skye!" The elves waved. They were still in shock that Santa was actually going. They thought he had been joking, but – no, he was going. He was gone. They were both gone.

Santa vanished out of sight as quick as a flash. The elves could no longer see him. They slowly walked back into the workshop with their heads down, scraping their feet in the snow. Not one elf made a sound or made a noise. There was complete silence.

The elves were now in the workshop at their work stations just looking and staring at each other, no one knowing what they should do. Should they just go back home? Should they have followed Santa and Mrs Claus to Scotland? They just didn't know what to do.

The oldest elf at the North Pole, whose name was Sualc (pronounced Su Alc), stood up and climbed onto a workbench in the workshop. Everyone immediately looked up to see what he was going to say and what he was going to do. Sualc, trying to think what he was going to say, started to speak. "Santa has now left the North Pole and it is unlikely that he will ever return again. We have never been in this situation before and this is new to all of us, as Santa's adventure is new to him. We have never done anything else before and I feel that we, the elves, need to do what we have always done."

"What's that?" an elf called out.

"We continue to build, build the toys for the boys and girls in the hope that Christmas will somehow continue. I don't know if it will continue in the way it has been done in the past but here, at the North Pole, the Christmas spirit lives through all of us and we all believe in Christmas. So we must, and we will, continue to build the toys," said Sualc.

There was pure joy at that moment in the workshop. "Christmas will go on!" called out the elves. The elves went to their workstations, getting all the tools and equipment they needed to build all the toys the boys and girls would need. There were so many different departments in the elves' workshop. There was the 'Electric and Gadget Department.' This is where all the computers, phones and all the other electronic devices you can think of were made. There was the 'Wheel Department.' This is where all the bikes, scooters, play cars and everything and anything you can think of that has wheels, were made. They had 'Softy Place.' This is where all the soft cuddly toys were made. There was the 'Arty-Elfy' Department. This is where all the arts and crafts were made. There were so many departments that the elves couldn't remember them all.

It had changed so much through the centuries. When they first started getting letters from the boys and girls, they didn't have that type, or sort, of demand for toys and presents. They only had three departments. They had:

1. The 'Fruit and Sweet Department.' This is where all the candy canes were made and where the oranges were planted and cared for.

2. The 'Toy Department.' This is where yo-yos, marbles, tin soldiers and skipping ropes were made.

3. The 'Bear and Doll Department.' This used to be the busiest department because these two toys used to be the most popular.

Now, instead of just having three departments, the North Pole workshop now had over one hundred different departments. There were more and more every year and the elves had to keep an eye on the new toys and gadgets that were being designed so that they could make them for the boys and girls. The elves were as busy as ever. The demand for different toys and gadgets was always increasing. It was good that the elves were exceptional at their job, otherwise there would have been a lot of unhappy boys and girls. When they started making the toys and gifts at the North Pole, there were only fifty elves but, after the last Christmas that had just gone, there were now over ninety thousand elves making them for all the boys and girls. That's a lot of elves and a lot of presents and gifts.

The elves weren't in the same happy, jolly, chirpy mood that they were usually in when they started making the toys at this time of year. They were sad, upset and struggling to have any Christmas spirit. Some of the elves were secretly questioning themselves about why they were making the toys this year because there was no Santa to deliver them. Some of the elves were hoping that, if they continued as normal, then their Christmas wish for Santa to return would come true and the toys and presents would get delivered as usual, like every other year. All the elves could do now was to wish and to hope that a Christmas miracle would come their way.

Chapter 5
New Job, New Career

Santa and Mrs Claus arrived in Skye in the early morning. It was a frosty and cold winter morning. It wasn't too cold for both of them, though. It was only -5 degrees Celsius. This was a heat wave for them. Santa circled the island of Skye. He was looking for the best place to land the reindeers, somewhere that they wouldn't be seen. Santa spotted an open patch of field that looked like a good place for them to land. He guided the two reindeers to the field where he needed to go. As they got closer to the ground, Santa called out "Easy, Comet. Easy, Cupid. Take it down slowly."

The sleigh and reindeers landed without a sound being made. They then came to a stop. Santa and Mrs Claus stood up and got out of the sleigh. They collected their bag that they had packed for their new beginnings. Santa walked around to Comet and Cupid, looked at both of them in their faces and put a hand on each of the reindeer's heads. Santa didn't speak for a few seconds. He just stood there with his eyes shut. He didn't know what to say. This would be the last time that he would see them. They were family. They were Santa's pets. It's just like you and me having a dog or a cat or any other animal you have as a pet. They were family to him. They meant so much to him. Santa spoke calmly and, with a tear running down his beard, he quietly said, "Thank-you for everything. I will always remember you and I will always remember all the days and nights that we rode together through the Christmas Eve sky. It is now time we say goodbye. You now need to go back home and help look after the elves."

At first Comet and Cupid did not move. They just stood there looking at Santa, with Santa looking at them. Comet and Cupid didn't want to go. They wanted to stay with them both. "You need to go now Comet, Cupid. Thank-you for bringing us here and we will miss each other but it really is time for you to go," said Santa.

Comet and Cupid bowed their head towards Santa. They then turned to the left and they started to walk, then trot, then canter, and then they went into a full gallop. Then they were off the ground and into the air. Within seconds, in the blink of an eye, they were up in the sky. The reindeers and sleigh could no longer seen in the clear morning sky. They had gone.

"Where to now? What do we do?" asked Mrs Claus.

"I think we should make our way to the village and see if we can find somewhere to live. We need to start planning and preparing what we are going to do," said Santa.

They started to walk across the field and then down the lane holding hands and walking towards the village. It was only a short walk to the village. During the walk, Santa and Mrs Claus never said a word to each other. The realisation of what they had done, and were doing, was starting to seem all too real for them now. They had left the North Pole. They had no elves, no reindeers and there was no more Santa.

They arrived in the village and agreed that the first thing they needed to do was to find somewhere that they could live. They walked around the village looking and trying to find somewhere to start their new life. They then came across an old tearoom cafe that was closed and boarded up. There was a sign on a board. It read "For Sale. If interested, or for any more information about this property, go to the estate agency located on the high street."

The building was small, but quaint – beautiful – but it needed a little bit of work doing. Santa was definitely not scared of a bit of work now, was he? He had previously done the hardest day's work that anybody had ever done, or could do.

"That's it, Mrs Claus. We need to go to the high street and see about purchasing this lovely building. Here is where our new life starts," said Santa.

"As long as you are sure, Mr Claus. If this is what you want, and what we need to do, then I'm happy for this to be our new life," said Mrs Claus.

They started walking, trying to find and locate the estate agent in the high street. They assumed that the high street would be near the seafront, so they headed that way. They could always ask someone for directions if they could not find it or if they got lost.

They found the estate agency as soon as they got onto the high street. They both stood outside for a couple of minutes, just looking at each other, not saying a word, just holding hands and both of them knowing that this was the start of their new life. They would be just like every other human in the world. No more magic and no more elves. It would be just the two of them from now on. They looked at each other and smiled. They both went inside the estate agency.

What a sight it must have been for the people in the office! A man and a woman that looked just like Santa and Mrs Claus in January had just walked in. What would they be thinking? What a sight it must've been, seeing those two standing there. It would definitely have raised some eyebrows and probably some questions.

"Hello there, sir, madam. How may I help you this morning?" a man's voice called out.

Santa approached the man and Santa began to speak. "Urm... We are interested in the property that is for sale in the village—the old tea rooms," Santa said, with a soft tone in his voice.

"Oh, right. Please take a seat," said the man. "I'm Mr Sevle and I will be able to help you with that."

Both Santa and Mrs Claus sat at a big desk. They looked a little bit uncomfortable, a bit nervous. This was all new to them. Mr Sevle looked at them both and said to them, "I hope you don't mind me saying this, but aren't you two a little bit late for dressing up for Christmas?"

"Oh..., oh..., no. We have just been on holiday to... to... to..." Mrs Claus was trying to think of somewhere. "...just came back from Canada where they celebrate dressing up at Christmas...and the best Santa and Mrs Claus look-alike win a prize—and we won," said Mrs Claus.

"We have just come from the airport and, when we arrived and went to collect our luggage, it had all gone missing. These are the only clothes we have to wear so we have had to continue to wear these until we get some more," said Mr Claus.

A big sigh was blown out by both Santa and Mr Claus. They had never thought about changing clothes.

"Well, congratulations on winning. Very well deserved, in my opinion," said Mr Sevle. "So—you are interested in purchasing the tearooms. Let me just get the details up on my computer. We have it listed for a very good price but it is also available to lease for twelve months. This lease can be extended every twelve months without any issues," said Mr Sevle.

Santa and Mrs Claus looked at each other and spoke to each other in a whispering manner. "What do you think? Shall we say twelve months and, if we like it, then we can stay here, or if we don't like it here we can move and look for something else," said Mrs Claus.

"Yes, that's a very good idea," said Santa. "We would like to lease it for twelve months please," said Santa.

"That's great. I'm sorry I never got your names, said Mr Sevle.

Santa and Mrs Claus had never even thought about changing their names. That had never crossed their minds.

"Well, my name…, my name is Nick. Yes. It's Nick," said Santa.

"My name is…" Mrs Claus was frantically trying to think of a name, any name. "My name is Merry," said Mrs Claus.

"Oh! Nice to meet you, Nick and Mary," said Mr Sevle. The estate agent thought that she had said her name was Mary. Mrs Claus was not going to tell him anything different. She just let him stick with Mary.

Santa explained to Mr Sevle that he would like to pay the full twelve-month lease on the property now. Mr Sevle said, "That is not a problem. We can do that. How would you like to pay? Will it be a card, cash or cheque?" Mr and Mrs Claus didn't even have a bank account so it wouldn't be a cheque or by card. It would have to be cash.

"We will pay you cash," said Mr Claus. But Santa had a problem. He couldn't remember what currency they used. He had never had to worry about money before.

Mr Sevle said, "That is perfect. That will be £1500 please."

What a relief that was. It wouldn't look so bad now for Santa. He didn't need to ask the embarrassing question. He opened his wallet and flicked through all the notes in his wallet. His wallet was the only magic thing he had brought with him. This would give him the money for any place in the world. No matter where he was or how much he wanted, it would be in there. "There you go, Mr Sevle", said Santa, as he handed over fresh, crisp clean notes.

"Thank-you."

Santa and Mrs Claus were starting to feel a little bit nervous now. Santa was wondering if had he given him the correct money. Had he accidentally given him the North Pole Snow Bank money?

"These are very new looking?" said Mr Sevle.

"Yes, we just exchanged them at the airport when we landed. We changed our winnings from the Santa look-alike competition we won. And I remember the lady saying that these are very new and crisp notes," said Santa.

Santa and Mrs Claus never realised that there would be so many questions. They hadn't really thought about anything. They never really planned for any of this. It was good that they could both think quickly to help them get out of any awkward questions that they were being asked.

They finally left the estate agent with the keys to the tearoom cafe, after what seemed like days of being in there. They made their way to the tearooms. When they got outside the tearoom cafe, they both stood there and looked at this small, beautiful building. "I know it's not what you are used to, Mrs Claus, but this is our new life now and, as long as we have each other by our side, this will work and we will be happy," said Mr Claus.

"Yes. This is true. Now, let's get inside and take a look," said Mrs Claus.

They entered the tearoom cafe through the side-door that had stairs leading to the upstairs. They both went in and went up the stairs. When they got to the top of the stairs, they were both pleasantly surprised by what they saw. It was a lovely open space. It had a kitchen, a living room, a bathroom, two bedrooms and a small door leading to the balcony that overlooked the sea. "This is perfect for us. It just needs a little bit of tidying and cleaning and we can call this place home," said Mrs Claus.

"Yes. You are right. Now, let's see if we can tidy this place up," said Mr Claus.

They both spent the rest of the day brushing, scrubbing, wiping, mopping and hoovering to make the place sparkle and gleam. They eventually finished late in the evening and then both settled down in the kitchen. "Do you want a drink?" asked Mrs Claus.

"Yes, please. I think I will. I will have one of your delicious Christmas hot chocolates that you make," said Santa.

Mrs Claus had already thought ahead. She had one ready and waiting for him. They both sat at the table. It was now time to start thinking of what they were going to spend their time doing. What job were they going to do? What job could they do? They both sat at the table discussing different ideas and jobs that could be possible.

"Postman," said Mrs Claus.

"No, Mrs Claus. I'm not built for all that walking. I only walk well in the snow," said Santa.

"Toy maker," said Mrs Claus.

"No. I don't think there are any toy making factories here in Skye," said Santa.

"Zoo-keeper. You could look after the reindeers and all the other animals," said Mrs Claus.

Santa had a quick look on the Skye map in the kitchen that had been left there by the previous owners. Santa looked and scanned the map. He looked all over the map. Then, Santa said, "That would be a great job but there are no zoos on the island. This is going to be harder than we first thought."

Santa sat back down at the table. He took a sip of his hot chocolate and then, all of a sudden, an idea hit him, an idea that had been staring at him in the face since he had first sat at the table. This was the best idea he had had, and it would be the best job for both of them. They would be able to live together, but they would also be able to work together. "I think I know what we can do for work Mrs Claus," said Santa.

"What's that?" said Mrs Claus.

"We have a tearoom below us that is not being used. We can open the tearoom up and we can sell your delicious hot chocolate," said Santa.

"What a fantastic idea! Yes—let's do it," said Mrs Claus, with excitement in her voice. She liked the thought of having more people enjoying and tasting her hot chocolate. It made her feel really happy. She liked making people happy.

Over the next couple of days, both Santa and Mrs Claus cleaned and tidied the tearoom. They painted and decorated it to make things just right, just how they wanted it to be, and with the right look. When the tearoom was completed, the transformation was amazing. The tearoom looked exactly like the tearoom from the North Pole, without realising what they had done. The warm sensation of home, the North Pole, went through both of them, and it raised a smile on their faces. They were happy. They both thought, "This is our new adventure, our new life—but with a hint of our old home."

The name above the tearoom had changed. It was no longer the tearoom. It was now called "The thorN loPe."

Chapter 6
Tea Rooms

The day was set for the grand opening of the thorN loPe. Both Mr and Mrs Claus had changed their appearance a little. They had changed out of their Santa and Mrs Claus clothes and they were now wearing more formal clothing. No kilts, though! Santa would not have looked good in one of those, not with his legs. He still kept his long white beard and he even wore his red hat. That was something he couldn't give up. The day started with a really slow influx of customers but, as the day went by, news started to get around the island about how good the hot chocolate was. Customers all loved the taste of it and some people had three or four cups of the hot chocolate before leaving. They all wanted to know, and have, the recipe, but Mrs Claus would not give up her secret to anybody. It had taken her a long time to get it right.

As the days went by, news got around the island about how good the hot chocolate was. More and more people began coming from all around just for the hot chocolate. People also loved how the thorN loPe looked. Drinking hot chocolate in a Christmas-themed room in the middle of February was awesome.

Their new work was a struggle at first for both Mr and Mrs Claus. They weren't used to working 5 days a week, 10 hours a day. It was too much sometimes. But, they finally got used to getting up in the morning, working all day and then enjoying the evening together. The North Pole very rarely crossed their minds because they were that busy but there would be the one odd occasion in the day when something would appear on TV that would remind them of their former home.

One evening, they were watching a programme called 'The reindeers of Lapland.' This made them start to think about Donner, Cupid, Comet and the rest of the herd. They started to think and wonder about what they were doing and what where they were getting up to. Sometimes, it brought a tear to their eyes when they started to think about the good times that they had had in the North Pole with the reindeers and the elves – but they were enjoying their new life that they had in Skye.

Before they knew what was happening, the days turned into weeks, the weeks turned into months and the months were going quicker than they thought they would've. Before they knew where they were, they were in September. Where was the time going? It was flying by really quickly. In the summer, the hottest time of the year, the people not only of Skye but the whole of the United Kingdom came to drink Mrs Claus's wonderful hot chocolate. People would come from miles around just to taste it. People never just wanted one. They wanted three, four and sometimes more. They just couldn't get enough of it. They loved it.

Business was going really well and they were starting to enjoy the life that they had now. Well – Mr Claus was enjoying life but Mrs Claus was starting to struggle. She didn't like the warm weather as much. She was missing the cold, the snow, the elves and the reindeers. She missed going out for walks in the snow, having snowball fights, building snowmen and making snow angels. She could no longer do this because the weather was warm. She hadn't seen any sort of snow since February and that snow was no match for the snow at the North Pole. That same evening, as Santa and Mrs Claus were relaxing outside sitting in the evening sun, Mrs Claus was quiet.

"What's wrong, my sweet?" asked Santa.

"I don't really know. I think I'm missing the North Pole more now than I have in all the time we have been here. I miss the elves. I miss some of the things like the cold." Mrs Claus was laughing as she said it.

"I am missing it too, Mrs Claus, but, as we know, the children of the world no longer need or appreciate us. It would be wrong to continue being Santa for there is no Christmas magic left. I'm sure the children will still get toys and presents at Christmas. Their parents will make sure they get something," said Mr Claus.

"Yes. You are right. I'll be OK. In the next couple of months, when the weather gets colder, it will cheer me up. I'm not a fan of this hot weather," said Mrs Claus. It was only 16 degrees Celsius but, to both of them, it felt like 40 degrees Celsius. They weren't used to any heat.

Mrs Claus and Mr Claus continued serving more and more hot chocolate through the months and, before they knew it, they were reaching the middle of November. There were only six weeks left until Christmas Eve. They never even realised at first but things were about to change.

Chapter 7
Appeals

It was getting closer and closer to December now and Santa could see the Christmas involvement within the village. People were starting to put up lights, Christmas trees, decorations and it was starting to snow. It was not like snow in the North Pole but there were flakes of the white stuff in the air. There were Christmas songs on the radio, carol-singers in the street and Christmas adverts on TV. The village was abuzz with excitement because Christmas was soon to be upon them. The children were getting all excited, thrilled that Santa would be coming soon, delivering the toys.

Santa was unaware of the children's excitement because he didn't see many children. Not many children came into the thorN loPe and he was too busy working, making hot chocolate for all his customers. Santa and Mrs Claus were busier than ever. They had to work longer hours and there were days when, after they had closed up, they went straight to bed. They were exhausted. Santa was enjoying seeing the carol-singers and hearing them sing their carols outside the thorN loPe, especially when they started to sing 'Santa Claus is coming to town.' Even though he was no longer Santa, that was still his favourite. It always put a smile on his face. Santa was busy. He was enjoying work and on Skye, he felt relaxed.

He had no hassle. This was his life now and he was enjoying it. He wasn't missing being Santa anymore.

During the following week, news started appearing all around the world. The news was that no one had heard of, or seen, Santa. They hadn't seen him in the sky practising his sleigh runs with his reindeers. They hadn't seen him in the shopping centres seeing children. There was nothing, not one sighting. The news reporter on the TV stated, "We have not had anyone in the world say that they have met or seen Santa this year. With Christmas hurriedly approaching, is this a time of concern? Will Santa appear in the next day or so? I believe that Santa is exceptionally busy at the North Pole ensuring that all the toys are ready to be delivered for Christmas. There are more and more children in the world now, so it just takes him longer to check the 'naughty and nice list' and make sure everything is ready. I will say now, on record, that Santa will show up in the next day or two and everything will be back to normal. We will all be laughing about this in a few days and saying that we have been worrying about nothing. This is El Leon reporting for TV1."

Santa had not seen any of the news. He'd seen no TV in days. He hadn't heard the radio or read a newspaper. He had just been too busy to take any notice of what was happening in the outside world. The customers who came into the shop didn't mention anything about what was going on. They didn't talk about Santa going missing or not being seen. They just wanted their hot chocolate. They came in for that and came in for that only. When they were drinking the hot chocolate, everything was great with them. It put a warm glow in them and everything in the world at that time was fine and perfect. There was nothing bad going on anywhere.

Mr and Mrs Claus sometimes wondered what the elves were up to in the North Pole and what adventures they were having. They were just wondering because they no longer had to make any toys. They wondered if they would ever come and visit them or if they were watching them on the Santa cameras. That was – if the cameras were still working. They might not be since Santa was no longer there. Had they visited them secretly, without them knowing? All they could do was wonder and imagine because they could no longer get in touch with the elves.

Santa carried on throughout the week, serving all the happy customers wanting the endless amounts of hot chocolate. "What did people drink before they moved here?" thought Santa. They went through gallons of the stuff and sometimes he and Mrs Claus only just had enough for the day. It was good that Mrs Claus stayed on top of the ordering.

Throughout the week there was more and more worrying news all over the world. Santa had still not been seen. There was not a "Ho! Ho! Ho!" anywhere to be heard. Not a red hat or white beard had been seen – nothing! The children of the world were starting to get a little bit more worried now. They started putting up posters in the windows at home, at school, at any places they went. The signs all had the same message: 'Has anyone seen SANTA? Where has he gone?' This happened in all of Europe, Africa, South and North America, Australia, Oceania and Asia. There was not a country, city, town or village without one of these signs in their windows. What had happened to him? Why had he not been seen? There were so many questions and most of the children were asking "Why…?" "Pour quoi…?" "Por qué…?" "Bakit…?" "Miksi…?" It was said in many languages around the world but everyone wanted to know the answer. They all wanted the same answer. They wanted Santa. Why was Santa not showing up anywhere? Where was he?

The news reporter was again on TV. This time he was looking and sounding a bit more anxious in his reporting. "This is El Leon reporting for TV1. I reported last week that Santa had not been seen anywhere in the world. We have all searched high and low, in the dry and in the snow. Letters have been sent by the boys and girls and still we haven't heard a word, seen a sleigh or even heard a jingle of any bells. I promised you this time last week that Santa would be here. But—here I am, still reporting that Santa has still not turned up. We need to continue to search, to pray and hope that Santa will appear again soon. Then Christmas will continue to be how Christmas should be—and that is with Santa. I hope to have better Christmas spirit news shortly but, for now, let's keep looking. This is El Leon signing off for TV1."

The adults of the world were also starting to get worried about Santa not being seen. Some of the adults were secretly writing letters to Santa, hoping that this would work. When they visited Santa with their children, they sometimes wished they could go and sit on his lap. They loved how Christmas and Santa made them feel. It brought out their inner child again. It reminded them of their Christmases when they were younger.

The children of the world were starting to get really worried now. They loved seeing Santa. They were missing him so much and they just wanted to know that Santa was OK. People around the world organised a Christmas song-singing party where, at the same time around the world, at 12pm GMT on December 1st, they would all go outside their homes, work, or wherever they were, and they would start to sing 'Santa

Claus is coming to town.' This was a worldwide phenomenon. It was made into a smash hit single and it was released into the music charts all around the world. It was Number 1 hit in 54 countries. All the money that was made went to charity. Even celebrities, singers, actors, sportspeople and politicians got involved. All the people of the world united. They were trying everything that they could think of to make Santa appear.

Still, Santa was oblivious to all what was going on. He just continued in the thorN loPe. He was enjoying his evenings at home and enjoying his time with Mrs Claus. Santa and Mrs Claus rarely ventured out anywhere. They stayed in their home and relaxed, enjoying each other's company. They were too tired to get out and about.

Chapter 8
No Belief

As the days went by, the adults and children began to lose what Christmas spirit they had left in them.

The adults and the children seemed to be more angry and upset with each other. There were more rows and arguments happening at home, at work – all over the place. No one seemed to be happy any more. No one was enjoying the holiday season that was quickly approaching. People were breaking up with each other. Partners leaving their partners, brothers their sisters, aunts their uncles, cousins their cousins, and – anyone else they knew. Rows would break out about the silliest things. They would stop talking to each other. It was such a strange atmosphere now in the world.

Children would be fighting in the playgrounds over Santa, with children laughing, teasing and mocking the children that still believed in Santa. They would say, "Told you, told you that Santa isn't real! The big fat man doesn't exist! Nah nah na na nah!"

The children that still believed continued to hope that Santa would turn up. They said, "Yes, he does exist. He is real and he will be here soon. You'll see. He will deliver all the presents to us. You'll see."

One boy who lived in Skye, Les Nit, loved Santa. He

loved Santa so much that he had pictures of him all over his bedroom. He had a Santa blanket and matching bedding on his bed. He had Santa teddies. His room was just full of Santa and Christmas stuff. He lived alone with his mom and they both loved everything about Christmas. Even through these strangest of times, they believed that Santa would still come. Most days after school, Les would come home crying, after hearing and listening to what the other children had been saying to him. He knew what they were saying was wrong but he didn't know what he could do to change their minds.

One afternoon, on the way home from school, Les walked past the thorN loPe. He walked past it every day. He loved the smell of the chocolate. He loved how it was decorated, all Christmassy. When he stared through the window at the two people who worked there, he just seemed to have a connection with them. They made him happy. He never went in. As much as he would have loved to go in, he just didn't. He loved hot chocolate but he and his mom could not afford one. His mom had recently lost her job and money was tight. They couldn't afford luxuries like that. Even if it was cheap, the money had to be spent elsewhere. He stood there, looking through the window. He thought to himself, "I will taste one of those hot chocolates one day. It may not be today or tomorrow, but, one day, I will."

He'd had a horrible day at school that day. The name-calling and the bullies made his life horrible. They teased him about having no dad, his mom having no job and how he still believed in Santa. He sat himself on the footpath just outside the thorN loPe. He sat there in silence. He started to cry, with tears starting to roll down his face. He was fed up. Why wouldn't the other children believe him that Santa was real? He knew that he was. He was sure that he had heard him and his sleigh a couple of Christmases ago but, by the time he got out of his bed and looked through the window, there was nothing. There was no sign of him, no sleigh and no reindeer. But – Les knew what he had heard.

Santa was working away in the thorN loPe. He looked out of the window and he noticed Les sitting on the footpath, all alone. He looked cold and upset. "One minute, Mrs Claus. I'm just popping outside to make sure Les is OK," said Santa.

"OK," replied Mrs Claus. Santa knew Les's name, even though they had never really officially met. That's one thing Santa knew. He knew every boy's and every girl's name in the world. That's one thing he would never forget. Santa went outside to Les. He sat down next to him and, in a quiet, relaxing, soothing voice, he said "What's wrong? It's the most wonderful time of the year. Christmas will soon be upon us and all the people are preparing themselves and getting everything ready for Christmas Day."

Les looked at Santa, and smiled. For some reason, Les felt something magical. He instantly stopped crying. There was something in this man's eyes that was calming. It made him feel that everything would be OK. "It's been a tough year, this year …so many changes," said Les.

"I know how you feel," said Santa.

"Well, at the beginning of the year my dad left home and he's not been back since, leaving me and my mom on our own. My mom then lost her job in the summer and we have been struggling ever since and, to top it off, there is mass panic everywhere in the world, as you probably know and have heard," said Les.

"Mass panic?" asked Santa.

"Yes. Everybody and everywhere all over the world people are in a panic—and me more than anyone," said Les. He was talking quicker and louder as he got closer to finishing his sentence.

"Calm down and talk slowly. Take a deep breath. Why is everybody panicking?" said Santa.

"Haven't you heard? You must have heard. It's been all over the news, on the TV, on the radio, and in all the newspapers. It's been everywhere! There have been signs and posters put in the windows of all the houses all over the world! Everyone knows about it or, to put it another way, no one knows anything about it," said Les.

"Now, this is getting a little bit confusing for me, Les? What has been going on? I've been working non-stop lately, seven days a week, twelve hours a day. I haven't had time to read, watch or listen to anything that has been going on in the world," said Santa.

"What do you mean you haven't seen or heard anything?" said Les, with a hint of surprise in his voice. At this point Les stood up. "Santa has DISAPPEARED!" shouted out Les.

Santa looked at Les. He was in shock. It took him a couple of seconds to take in what Les had just said to him. Had he really heard what he had said? "Can you repeat what you just said, please, Les?" said Santa, trying to gather his thoughts and trying to take in what Les had just told him.

"Santa has disappeared. No one has seen or heard from him. Not one single 'HO! HO! HO!' anywhere. He's gone and I'm worried and…, and…, and…, hang on a minute! How do you know my name? I never told you my name," said Les.

Santa paused for a second. He was in shock and taken aback. People were missing him. People did need and appreciate him.

Santa got up, looked at Les and said, "Thank-you." He said nothing more. He just walked back into the thorN loPe. Les stood there. He didn't know what to say or do. He looked in the window and saw Santa and Mrs Claus talking. He couldn't hear what they were saying but they had switched on the TV. Les just shrugged his shoulders and walked off home.

Chapter 9
Open Mouthed

Santa walked into the thorN loPe, trying to stay as calm as possible. The shop was empty now. He closed the door behind him and locked it. Mrs Claus had a puzzled look on her face. Santa had never closed the shop this early before. "What's up with you, Mr Claus?" asked Mrs Claus.

Santa stood there for a few seconds. He walked over to the TV and switched it on. "I think we need to see what's going on in the outside world," said Santa.

"What's happened? Tell me what you have seen. What have you heard?" said Mrs Claus.

"I... I just need to watch this. I think we both need to watch this. Something is happening all over the world. I think I may have made a massive mistake," said Santa.

"What mistake?" said Mrs Claus.

Santa never spoke a word and, for the next 30 minutes, Mr and Mrs Claus watched countless TV shows, adverts and news channels. It was the same on every channel. Different people were asking the same question: "Where is Santa?" There were numerous people coming up with reasons and answers for why Santa had disappeared. Neither of them could believe what they were watching. They just stood there with their mouths open, not saying a word and with a look of shock on their faces. What were they seeing? What were they watching? This couldn't be happening! At this point, Santa realised that he had got it all wrong. He was really, really wrong.

Santa turned the TV off and sat on a chair at one of the tables. Mrs Claus just stood there looking at the TV. Even though the TV was turned off, she was just standing there, trying to take everything that she had just seen on TV in. Was this really happening? She finally turned around and saw Santa with his head on the table muttering to himself. He just kept repeating the same thing over and over to himself. "What have I done?"

Mrs Claus walked over to Santa and placed a hand on his shoulder, trying to reassure him. She spoke softly, "What are we going to do? The children of the world do need you. We need to get back to the North Pole somehow to try and save Christmas."

"How are we going to do that? We are stuck here. We have no way of contacting the elves, calling the reindeers—nothing," said Santa. He was getting more and more stressed the more and more he thought about what he had seen. Now, panic was starting to set in. His voice was a tremble when he spoke. He was starting to hyperventilate.

"Calm down, Mr Claus. You need to keep calm. We will think of a way we can get you back to the North Pole. Let's just stay calm," said Mrs Claus. They started thinking of ways they could get back to the North Pole, trying to think of different ways of getting back.

"I can walk it back," said Santa.

"You can't walk it. Christmas Eve is only three weeks away and you will never make it," said Mrs Claus.

"I can. I can... I can swim it to the North Pole from here. I will do that," said Santa.

"I'm not even going to answer that, Mr Claus. That will be ridiculous. You can't even swim," said Mrs Claus.

"I will get a plane from the mainland and I can fly there," said Santa. He was trying desperately to think of ways of getting back to the North Pole – anything, anyhow, anyway.

"There are no planes that go to the North Pole and, if a plane did take you there, there is no runway for the plane to land. And —what are you going to say to the pilot? Are you just going to land there, by the igloo village but make sure you avoid the toy workshops that you can't see?" said Mrs Claus.

"There must be a way that I can get back to the North Pole. There's got to be a way. I just need to clear my head and think sensibly about this," said Santa.

Santa and Mrs Claus thought long and hard about how they were going to solve the problem that they were facing. Santa started pacing around trying hard to think of something – anything – just hoping that some idea would come up. He looked out of the window and, suddenly, he saw a way, the only way he could get back to the North Pole. There, outside in the near distance was the answer he had been looking for – a boat. He could catch a lift with a fisherman and he could ask him to take him there on his trip out to sea. Santa explained his idea to Mrs Claus. She agreed that this was the best option for him to get back to the North Pole. It was the best, and only, option that he had."

Mrs Claus then explained to Santa that it was too late to go now and that he would have to go first thing in the morning. "You will need to have a good night's rest and we will have to hope that you make it back in time for you to sort out Christmas and presents for the children."

Santa was searching on the internet at this point to find out how far away the North Pole was and how long it would take him to get back to the village. He started looking for boats, ships – for anything that would be going to the North Pole. After searching for a short while, he found a boat that would set off tomorrow at 6 am. It would take him eleven days to travel the two thousand miles he needed to get there. It would then be another two-day walk to get to the North Pole village. Then, he would have just seven days to get everything sorted before Christmas Eve. This would have to work. It had to work. It was the only option that they both had.

Mr Claus explained it all to Mrs Claus and she agreed that this was the best and only option that they had. "I just need to make sure the presents are all ready." Suddenly, Santa realised he had forgotten about the most important aspect of his job, the presents. "What am I going to do for presents? What am I going to deliver? They will just have to have a basic toy. Will they be OK with the basic toys from years ago? It will need to be teddy bears, dolls, a tin soldier or a yo-yo for them. I won't have time to give them the presents that they have asked for. Will the elves still be there? The only way I will know and find out the answers to all these questions is when I get back to the North Pole," said Santa.

Santa then explained to Mrs Claus that he would pick her up when he delivered the presents to the children on Skye on Christmas morning. Mrs Claus agreed to this. This was the best thing to do. She didn't want to slow him down in getting back to the North Pole.

Now, Santa had to pack everything that he was going to need for his long trip. He started to think about the sort of things he was going to need. He would need food, drinks and clean clothes. He would then need additional items for his two-day walk in the North Pole. He'd need a tent, a compass, a torch, ski shoes – there was so much he would need. He wanted to make sure that he had everything he needed. He couldn't rely on the Christmas magic that he usually had. He had none, not until he got back to the North Pole. Santa packed his bag and was ready to get going. He wanted to save Christmas. He had to. This was his mess that he had created and it was only he who could save Christmas.

That night, Santa didn't really sleep. He had too much on his mind. There were too many things going around his head and so many questions. He just kept thinking, "What if I don't get back in time? I will have ruined everybody's Christmas. Will I make it back? Will the elves still be there? Will I get delayed on the boat? Will I ruin Christmas?" He just couldn't settle and relax. He couldn't believe how wrong he had been and that he was still needed and appreciated, not only by the children but also the adults.

The following morning arrived within a blink of an eye. Santa had only managed a couple of hours' sleep but he was up and ready to return to the North Pole. Santa and Mrs Claus hugged and shared a warm embrace. Santa picked up his bag and started to walk off towards the harbour. Mrs Claus waved him off and, as Santa wandered off into the distance, she called out to him, "See you soon. Stay safe," and "I'm missing you already," and "Don't forget to collect me Christmas Eve!"

Santa just waved back and carried on walking. He then shouted back to her, "I won't forget you."

Santa arrived at the docks and he started looking for the boat and the fisherman that could take him back to the North Pole. He finally found the boat he was after in the harbour. Its name was 'H C Nirg.' Santa called out to see if anyone would answer. He called a couple of times, "Hello, is there anybody there?"

A man finally appeared on deck. "Are you going by the North Pole?" asked Santa. "I am," answered the man.

"Can I jump aboard and join you? I'm in desperate need to get to the North Pole. I have an urgent job to complete and don't have a lot of time to do it. I need to save Christmas," said Santa.

The man laughed at Santa and shouted back to him, "No way are you getting on my boat! I don't care about Christmas, never have and never will!" The boat then started off and pulled away and out to sea.

Santa then realised who the man was. He remembered him as a boy. He was the boy who was never once on the nice list. He was the only child in the history of him being Santa that had been on the naughty list thirteen years in a row. His name was Ego Orcs.

Santa started frantically searching for boats, any boats, ships, yachts, vessels, – anything that was going near, or to, the North Pole. He started asking different fishermen, sailors and boat people. Anyone who was with a boat, in fact. He would ask them all the same question, "Are you going to the North Pole?"

But he kept getting the same answer. "No, sorry."

Santa got more and more concerned that he wasn't going to get back. He reached the last boat in the harbour. This was his final hope of getting back to the North Pole. The boat was called 'Flodur.' He saw the captain standing on the boat looking out to sea. Santa shouted out to him, "Excuse me! Are you going anywhere near the North Pole?"

The man looked down at him, took his pipe out of his mouth and answered, "Well, actually, I'm about to leave port in the next ten minutes. What do you want to go to the North Pole for, matey?" said the captain.

Santa hadn't thought about a reason to tell people why he was going to the North Pole. He quickly had to think of something. "Urm... I'm going because... because... it's always been an ambition of mine to reach the North Pole and this is the year I'm going to do it. I want people to do things regardless of their age. If they set their mind to something then they can do anything," said Santa.

The captain looked down towards Santa and a smile appeared on his face. "Jump on board ship, mate—happy to have you on board," said the captain.

Santa climbed up onto the boat and was met by the captain. "Hi! I'm Fle Sam X and I'm happy to meet you," said the captain.

Santa shook Fle's hand and replied, "Happy to meet you and season's greetings to you. Thank-you for helping me on my adventure and my quest to get to the North Pole. I really appreciate you helping me like this," said Santa.

"You are more than welcome. But—sorry, I didn't quite catch your name," said Fle.

"Oh! Sorry, I'm San..." Santa suddenly stopped what he was about to say. "I'm Nick. it's good to know, and meet you, too," said Santa.

Fle showed Santa where he could put his bag. Fle then explained to Santa why he was sailing up to and around the North Pole. He was on an adventure of his own. Fle explained to Santa that he was a scientist who was interested in looking at the local wildlife around the area of the North Pole. He wanted to see how the wildlife behaved around Christmas time – to see if there was anything true in what people had told him. People had said that the wildlife was different because of the 'Santa-effect.'

"The 'Santa-effect!' What's the Santa-effect?" asked Santa.

Fle started to explain. "During the run up to Christmas there seems to be more and more wildlife activity in the North Pole, more than any other time of the year. There are more polar bears, more walruses, more penguins, whales – you name it. The animals that like the cold weather seem to group together at the North Pole. I want to see if there is any logical reason for this."

Santa turned away and smiled. As he walked away, he muttered, "I know the answer to your question."

"Did you say something, Nick?" asked Fle.

"No. Nothing, replied Santa.

Chapter 10
Exploration Home

The boat left the island of Skye. The sea was quite calm. The sea is a place where you can think and reflect on things. It can be peaceful. You gather your thoughts and clear your head to put things into perspective. Santa was just hoping that he would get home in time. He really needed to sort out the mess he had created.

Santa was given a cup of tea from Fle. "Here you go, Nick," said Fle. Santa took the drink from Fle and he took a sip. It wasn't the best cup of tea he'd ever had but, seeing where they were in the middle of the sea, it would do.

"How long do you think it will take us to get to the North Pole?" asked Santa.

"Well, the weather is going to be a bit choppy and rough over the next few days, so that may delay us a little, but we will get there. I'm sure we will get there in ten or eleven days' time. I hope this will be OK for you."

"Yes. That will be perfect," said Santa.

Fle then started to explain to Santa why he wanted to go to the North Pole. "I decided that this was the year I was going to go to the North Pole. It's a place I've always wanted to go, winter seems to be the best time to see all the wildlife around the North Pole. The stories, the videos and the pictures I've seen are amazing. I just wanted to see it. I can't wait to see it for myself," Fle said.

"It is—you will love it," said Santa, smiling like a Cheshire cat.

"It is what?" asked Fle.

"It is… it is… it is going to be a nice ten or so days on this boat with you. I'm as excited as you about you doing your adventure as I am to be doing my adventure," said Santa, quickly thinking of something to say. Santa quietly reminded himself that he needed to be a little more careful about what he said to Fle. He didn't want to let it slip that he was Santa.

The next week at sea went really quickly. The sea was rough. There were a lot of waves crashing against the boat. Santa found it really tough at first. He didn't like the motion of the boat – up and down, side to side, over big waves, through the waves and the sea water splashing in his face. He found it tough. On a few occasions, he was seasick. It was not a pretty sight, as you can imagine. He was just glad that he didn't have to do this all the time. He was thankful that he had his reindeers and he flew on Christmas Eve.

As the trip went on, Santa got better with the sea. He was secretly beginning to enjoy it once the sea sickness had passed. He started to realise why people enjoyed the sea and why they would spend days, weeks and months out at a time. It was a fantastic place to be.

Santa started to realise at this point that he had better come up with a plan of action for when he returned to the North Pole. He needed to write down what he was going to do and what he needed to do. He got his Santa book and pen out of his bag and placed it on the table. The book was centuries old. This is where Santa kept all his memories of all the good times that he had had, and where he wrote down the things he wanted and needed to remember. Well, how else was he going to remember everything that he had done? Sometimes he couldn't even remember what he went into the kitchen for!

Santa started talking to himself and he began to make a list of what he was going to do, trying to make sure that he had remembered everything. He didn't want to forget anything. He wanted to make sure that he saved Christmas. He started to write a list of what he needed to do:

1. Get to the North Pole before Christmas Eve. Well, that was the most important thing to do. If he couldn't do this then he couldn't complete the rest of this list, he thought.

2. Find the elves. If they had left the North Pole, he would need to find where they had gone.

3. Sort out presents for the children if the elves could not be found.

4. Check the list twice (you know, THAT list – everyone knows about that list – the 'naughty and nice' list). He would have to read it quicker than he had ever read it before and then read it again, even more quickly than he had the first time.

5. Take the reindeers on a test run. They hadn't done any proper flying or practice runs all year.

6. Fill the sleigh with gifts and presents and to be ready to go on Christmas Eve, making sure there is at least one toy, gift or present for all the children on the nice list.

7. Deliver the presents to the children of the world.

8. Return home.

"That's it. The list is all done. It's going to be a rush but I can do it. I know I can do it. Well—I have to do it," said Santa, speaking to himself.

Santa looked pleased with himself that he now had a

plan of action and now that he knew what he had to do. He was looking forward to getting Christmas done and returning home to the North Pole, to Mrs Claus and her delicious hot chocolate. A thought then entered Santa's head, a sort of panic, a sort of reminder, like something else that he needed to do. It was something so important and he hadn't made a note of it on his list. "Oh no! How can I forget that for my list? If I forgot that, I would be in big trouble," said Santa, as he spoke out aloud to himself. He added the reminder to his list in big bold capital letters. 7B. COLLECT MRS CLAUS FROM SKYE. How could he forget Mrs Claus? He had so many things, so many thoughts and ideas going around his head, that he was just worried. He wanted to make sure that he had everything right. He didn't want to forget anything. So, he decided to do something else, something that he thought was right and the best thing to do. He decided that he would check his list twice, just like he did with the naughty and nice list.

Everything was now ready for Santa. He just needed to get back to the North Pole to start his tasks and to save Christmas.

One morning, Santa was suddenly awoken by Fle. "Nick, it's time to get up. We have arrived. We are at the North Pole."

Santa jumped out of bed, got himself dressed and made sure that he was wrapped up nice and warm. He had so many warm layers on him that it made him look like he had balloons up his clothes. He was like a big inflatable. Fle got him as close as he could to land but he knew that he would not be able to dock the boat. "You will have to jump into that dingy and row yourself the rest of the way. It's only a couple of metres but you will be OK to do it," said Fle.

"Thank-you for everything that you have done for me and I will never forget it. You are a true friend and you have done more to help save Christmas than you think, or could ever have imagined," said Santa.

Fle had a surprise look on his face. "What do you mean I've saved Christmas?" said Fle.

Santa put his hand on his shoulder and spoke softly and said, "You are a nice man. I have to complete my work here and me being here will allow me to sort out the deliveries that need making," explained Santa.

Fle was still a little bit surprised. He didn't quite understand what Nick had just said to him. Fle thought he was here to reach the top of the North Pole, not to do any deliveries. He just shrugged his shoulders. Fle shook Santa's hand and wished Santa well. Santa climbed into the dingy and wished Fle all the best on his adventure and hoped he would find the answers he was looking for. Santa then started to row to shore. They both waved to each other and wished each other a Happy Christmas. Santa thought to himself as he started to row the dinghy, "It will only be a happy Christmas if I can reach the North Pole before Christmas Eve, which is in nine days' time."

It took Santa only ten minutes to row to shore. He rowed as quickly as he could. He didn't have time to waste. He pulled the dinghy on to the shore, dragged it and placed it on the snow. He put the oars into the dinghy and started to get his stuff out the bag that he would need. He put on his ski-shoes and he started off on his long two-day walk. It had just started to snow and visibility was poor. He could just about see his hand in front of his face.

Santa reached into his pocket and he pulled his torch and compass out to ensure he knew where to go and to make sure he was going the right way. He looked at the compass. He needed to walk north and he needed to walk fifty miles from his current location. He was indeed going in the right direction so he knew that he was off to a good start. Santa was quite good at walking in the snow. He had many years of doing this. He would have to walk at least twenty-five miles a day. It shouldn't be a problem. Santa put his torch and compass away. He started walking again and soon he was going at a good pace. You would actually have thought that he was jogging rather than walking because he was walking that quick. Before he knew it, Santa had walked thirty miles, five miles more than he needed to have done. "That's a good day of walking, I think it's time to stop," said Santa to himself.

Santa set up his tent. He was ready for a well-deserved rest. He got his sleeping bag out, poured himself a drink and had something to eat. He only had orange squash and a ham sandwich. That would have to do for him. Well, there is no cafe, burger restaurants or anything like that in the North Pole to go and visit. Well, there is – but only Santa knew about it and, anyway, it was twenty miles away in the village and only Santa and the elves could see it. Santa settled down for the night and, in a blink of an eye, he was fast asleep. He started dreaming about everything that he was going to do when he got to the village and how he was going to save Christmas and deliver all the presents to the children.

Then, all of a sudden, his dreams started to turn into nightmares. He started to see visions where he got stuck in a snowstorm. Then he got lost. Then, when he finally got to the village, it was deserted – no elves, no presents, nothing, no one. He then went to the reindeers. They were there but they were all over-weight. They were in no shape to stand, let alone fly. Santa woke up suddenly. He sat bolt upright. He was sweating. He said, "That will not happen. I will get to the village and everything will be OK. I will deliver the presents on Christmas Eve."

Santa packed up all his stuff and took down the tent. He was now ready for the last twenty miles. Santa was determined. He was ready to complete his walk and get back home to the village. He began walking as fast as ever. Nothing was going to stop him. Nothing would dare get in his way. His mind was set and he knew he would, and could, do it. Santa walked and walked and walked and walked and, before he knew it, he could see where he needed to be. He was metres away from the village. He just hoped that everything was OK.

He got to the magic door of the village. When you look at it, it looks just like snow and ice but, if you look at the right angle, you can see the door to the most magical place in the world.

Santa opened the door. He stepped through, closing the door behind him. His worst fears seemed to be happening right in front of him. There was no one around. He couldn't see anybody, not an elf, a reindeer – nobody, nothing. It was quiet and lifeless.

He continued to walk around the village. He couldn't find or see anybody. He finally made it to the workshop. He was trying to figure out how he was going to sort out all the toys and everything else that was on his list.

Santa opened the door to the workshop and he was completely surprised by what he saw in front of him. He couldn't believe it. He started to cry and he fell to his knees. This could not be happening. He thought, "What am I seeing? This can't be real!"

Chapter 11
Let's Get To Work

Santa couldn't believe it. All the elves were there. They were there sorting all the presents out. They were making presents. They were getting ready for Christmas. They were completing, building, wrapping and sacking all the presents that the children wanted. "How have you managed to do this?" called out Santa. The elves were so busy in their work that they had never even seen Santa enter the workshop. They all stopped what they were doing. They looked up. Were they dreaming? Was this real? Was Santa really there? They all stood up in silence, still in shock that Santa was there. They had hoped that he would return before Christmas Eve and there he was, standing there right in front of their eyes. He was back. The elves all cheered and they ran over to Santa. All of them were crying and trying to hug Santa. They had all missed him and Santa had missed them just as much. He was home.

The elves suddenly broke out into song. "Santa will be riding on his sleigh." They all sang at the top of their voices.

Then, Santa took over. "I'm making a list. I'm going to be checking it twice. I......... am coming to town!" They all stopped and cheered. Then Santa spoke. "It's so good to be back, elves. I've missed you so much. I'm so sorry. I made a big mistake. The children do need and believe in me. They love us all at the North Pole. I must save Christmas but we have so much work to do and we only have seven days to do it."

"Don't worry, Santa. We have prepared and done as much as we can. Now, it's your time to rock and roll the show," said a voice in the crowd. Santa couldn't quite see who it was who had said it. "I will update you and tell you what we have done and what you need to do next, Santa," said the same voice. Still, Santa couldn't find out where the voice was coming from.

"Who's that speaking? said Santa. The elf stepped forward. Santa could now see who it was. There in front of him was Sualc. "Thank-you, Sualc. Thank-you for everything you have done," said Santa.

"Now is not the time for 'thank-yous'. You can do that later. We have Christmas to save. Follow me and I can show you what needs doing," said Sualc.

Santa followed Sualc into the chimney room and what he saw shocked him. There were letters in the room from floor to ceiling – wall to wall. There was one small space where you could get to the chair by the fireplace and nothing else. There were thousands and thousands of letters. Santa had never seen this number of letters ever.

"This isn't all of them. There are more, a lot more. We have had to put the rest of the letters in the library. We had to take all the books out and put them in there," said Sualc.

Santa couldn't believe what he was seeing and hearing. "The children of the world do appreciate and need me. How could I have been so wrong? Where do I start? Where do I begin with all these letters? How do I know what each child wants? How will I do it all in only seven days? Reading the letters wasn't even on my list of things to check and do. I didn't think there would be any," said Santa.

Santa started to look around and he picked a couple of letters up and started to read them.

"Dear Santa,

I have been very good this year and I would like a bicycle and a new phone, please. Love Casper. Aged 8. New York, U.S.A."

"Querido Papa Noel,

Me he esforzado mucho por ser bueno este año. A veces he sido horrible con mi hermana, pero he hecho todo lo posible por ser buena. Quisiera una muñeca y un poco de maquillaje por favor. Gracias.

(Dear Santa, I have tried very hard to be good this year. Sometimes I have been horrible to my sister, but I have tried my best to be good. I'd like a doll and some make-up please. Thank you).

Natalina, 10, Barcelona, Espana (Spain)."

"Dear Santa,

Merry Christmas. I want lots of things for Christmas. I know you know what I want so I don't need to ask. Love Holly, 6, England."

This letter made Santa laugh and chuckle. In the height of all this and, despite how overwhelming the task was going to be, this made him smile. He then read one more letter.

"Santa, I hope you are OK. I am really worried that something may have happened to you. I hope you receive this letter and you are safe and well. I do not want anything for Christmas this year – no toys, no games, nothing. There are only two things I want. They are for you to be OK and that you get to deliver all the presents this year because nobody has seen or heard from you. The other thing is that I want my mom to be happy. I want her to get a job. She has tried so hard but she doesn't seem to get anything. I know this may be difficult for you as you deliver and make presents but, if you could make this come true, I will be truly thankful.

From Les Nit, aged 9 and half, Skye, Scotland."

Santa couldn't believe that out of all the letters he could've read he had picked Les's letter. "This is it. Somehow, some way I am going to be ready to go Christmas Eve," said Santa.

"Well, I think I may have made your sorting out a little bit easier," said Sualc.

"Why? What have you done? asked Santa.

"Well, I have read all the letters that have been sent. I have arranged for all the toys and gifts to be made and prepared. Most of the presents have been wrapped and bows have been put on them and they have been placed ready into the sack for Christmas Eve. We only have a million presents and gifts left to make and prepare but we should have all of them ready before Christmas Eve's flight," said Sualc.

"Wow! Wow! And… wow! Thank-you Sualc. Thank-you to all the elves. You are all fantastic and thank-you for carrying on, for still believing in me, believing in Santa, and still having the Christmas spirit. Thank-you for continuing to make the toys and gifts and knowing that I would return. You knew and I didn't," said Santa, again hugging Sualc.

Santa then got his check list out of his bag and he started to read it. "Number 1. Go to the North Pole. Well, that's done. I can tick that one off. Number 2. Find the Elves. Well, I think I have that one done, and I have found you all, which is a big relief, I can tell you. Number 3. Check the 'naughty and nice' list. That's what I need to do now. For the next couple of days, I will have to read and read and read again. Then, when I have finished, I will need to read and read and read again, so I will have checked it twice," said Santa.

Santa grabbed the two books from the chimney room and he made his way to his comfy chair in the kitchen. This is where he was going to check his list, not once, but twice.

As he got to the kitchen and sat down, he suddenly felt tired. He was too exhausted and tired after the day's walk and everything else that had happened since he had returned to the village. Since he had returned to the village, he'd seen the elves, found out all the letters had been looked at and sorted, and he didn't need to make any of the gifts or presents for the children – thanks to the elves – but, more importantly, he discovered that a lot more was done than he thought would need doing. He had less work to do. Santa yawned. It was the biggest yawn anybody has ever done. He was tired. It was time for him to go to bed. "One more day won't hurt. I need to rest now. There are going to be busier days that lay ahead for me, and I need to make sure I'm not too tired to do them," Santa said, as he talked to himself.

Santa slept well. He enjoyed being back in his own comfy big bed. The following morning, he was awoken by Sualc. "Time to get up, Santa, time to start checking the list," said Sualc.

"I will. I'm getting up right away," said Santa.

Sualc had just thought about something. "Where is Mrs Claus? He asked.

"Well, she is still in Skye. I left her there and told her that I would collect her on Christmas Eve when I deliver the presents to the children in Skye," said Santa.

"Oh. That was a good idea. I can't wait to see her. I've missed her," said Sualc.

"Neither can I. I'm missing her too," said Santa.

For the next two days, Santa read the 'naughty and nice' list. "Emily—nice.

Maisie—nice.

Charlie—naughty. But I think he may sneak onto the 'nice' list the second time I check it."

The second time Santa checked it, he was reading out loud again.

"Emily—nice.

Maisie—nice.

Charlie—nice.

I knew Charlie would turn it around. He always does this. He has his flaws but he's a good boy really."

Santa had checked the list and he had checked it twice. The 'naughty and nice' list was all done. "Another job on my checklist is done What now?" Santa asked himself. Santa took the list out again. He crossed out Number 3 on the checklist. "I'm getting through the list. There are only three days left now until Christmas Eve. What's next?" he asked himself. Santa looked at the list. "Number 4. Take the reindeers on flying test runs. I had better get myself dressed. I hope they can still fly?" said Santa.

Santa suddenly had a fear that they wouldn't be able to fly after not doing any exercise or flying for nearly a year. Santa got himself ready and he hurried himself over to the reindeer stable. Santa went into the stable and found that all the reindeers were asleep. They were all fast asleep. Santa knew how to wake them. So, at the top of his voice, he started to call out, "On Dasher! On Dancer! On Prancer! On Vixen! On Comet! On Cupid" On Donner" On Blitzen!" And... "On Rudolph!" The reindeer were startled. They woke up a bit groggy. They started looking around wondering what was going on. Then, they all spotted him in the doorway. It was Santa! He'd come back.

The reindeer galloped quickly towards Santa. In doing so, they knocked him to the ground – accidentally, of course. They were all licking him, rubbing their nose in his cheeks and trying to show how much they had missed him. "Hang on boys and girls. I take it you've missed me," Santa said, trying to stand up. "Well, I've missed you all too. Who's up for a couple of days of flying to get us all into shape and to be ready for Christmas Eve?" Santa asked them. All the reindeer stamped with excitement. They all lined up, ready to be harnessed to the sleigh.

Santa harnessed the reindeers and the sleigh. They were ready to go. He got in the sleigh and held the reins. "Are you ready?" called out Santa. Before he could say another word, the reindeers shot out of the stable, quicker than they had ever galloped before. Like a flash they were in the sky. It was just like they had always done it. They had missed flying, just as much as Santa had missed it.

Santa flew them all day and, the following day, the reindeers were ready to go and so was Santa. Another thing completed on the checklist. Santa was happy that he was getting what he needed doing, done, but he knew he couldn't have done it without the elves. He was pleased that they had carried on as normal without him.

The following morning Santa got up. He was again woken up by Sualc. "Good morning, Santa," said Sualc. Santa woke up wiping his eyes. The last couple of days had started to catch up with him and he was a little more tired than usual.

"Is everything OK?" asked Santa.

"Well, I think we may need your help, Santa. We have still got one hundred thousand toys and gifts left to make, wrap and get ready to go in the sleigh. More and more children have written to you this year wanting presents. They have been worried about you. They thought that, by writing to you, they would make you appear, and they would see you. We need your help now Santa," said Sualc.

Santa jumped out of bed, put on his clothes and was ready. "Just bear with me I will be with you in five minutes. I just need to have a wash and brush my teeth. I don't want my teeth going bad, having bad breath and being smelly now, do I?" explained Santa.

Sualc smiled and said, "Yes—you are right. No matter how much something needs doing, you must make sure you stay clean and healthy."

Santa made his way into the workshop and asked Sualc what he wanted him to do.

"Santa, I need you to make phones for the children. We need hundreds of these," said Sualc.

"No problem. Leave this with me and I will take care of it. Are you OK dealing with everything else, Sualc?" asked Santa.

"That's great. And, yes, I will be able to deal with everything else. I will let you know if I need you for anything," said Sualc.

Santa got on with making the phones. He was good at making them and making them quickly too. That's why Sualc had given this job to Santa. He could make three phones quicker than an elf could make one.

The elves and Santa worked all day and well into the night. They had finally got everything done in the early hours of the morning. Santa went and collected the sack of presents. He started to fill the sleigh with the presents and the sack. The sleigh looked empty compared to all the presents that had been made, but the sack was a magic Christmas sack. The toys and presents shrunk to nearly nothing. Santa was the only one that could see them inside the sack. This was the only way that he could get all the presents and gifts to fit into his sleigh.

Well, could you imagine how many reindeers and how big the sleigh would need to be to deliver the presents if they stayed their normal size? It would be bigger than anything you have ever seen. The weight of the presents would be too heavy for the sleigh and it would probably break. Then, the reindeers wouldn't be able to get themselves, or the sleigh, off the ground.

The sleigh was finally done and ready, all packed to go. Santa had to start delivering the presents in just twelve hours' time. "I just need to check my checklist to see what I have to do next," said Santa. He looked at his list. Numbers 1, 2, 3, and 4 were already ticked off. Number 5 was now done; the sleigh was all ready to go. Number 6. Deliver presents. And, Number 7. Return home. That's it. I'm all done and ready for tomorrow. Oh, and, yes—Number 7b. Collect Mrs Claus," said Santa. Santa was happy that he was ready to deliver all the presents and he was going to save everybody's Christmas, with the help of the elves. It was now time for him to get some sleep. He had a busy day and night coming up. He needed to rest.

Santa was just about to settle down and relax in his bed and get off to sleep when he started to think about all those letters that had come but, especially, the one he got from Les. He got out of his bed, went to his desk and he started to write a letter. Then he wrote another one and then, one more. He placed them into envelopes and put them in his pocket jacket of his Santa suit. Santa then returned to his bed and went to sleep.

Santa woke after eleven hours of good uninterrupted sleep. He showered, washed and brushed his teeth until his teeth were glowing like the white snow outside. He was all suited and booted with his Santa suit on. He was really happy that he was Santa again. He loved being Santa again. If someone had asked, or told him, six months ago if he would've been doing this, he would have said, "No. I'm not wanted, needed or appreciated. The children no longer need, believe in or want Santa." How wrong he was! But here he was, fixing his wrong.

Santa made his way to the stables where he harnessed the reindeers to each other and to the sleigh. Santa was all ready to go. The reindeers were ready, the sleigh was ready – and the elves? Well, they had always been ready. Santa got into his sleigh, pulled on the reins and shouted, "Let's go and deliver Christmas!" The reindeers flew out of the stables so quickly, faster than a rocket. They were in a hurry. They wanted to save Christmas but they also wanted to collect Mrs Claus. They had also missed her.

Chapter 12
Fly My Reindeers

Santa steered the sleigh. Flying the reindeers through the night sky, he called out to them, "First stop, the Pacific Ocean, the South Pacific." Santa reached the Pacific Ocean in record time. He delivered all the presents and gifts to the children in Australia in the quickest ever time. He really was flying. Well, of course he was. He had his reindeers. He was now set for Japan, then through the rest of Asia, across to Africa, up to Europe, across the Atlantic Ocean to Canada, USA, Mexico and then, finally, Central and South America. He would be finished before he knew it.

He had completed Asia, Africa, Eastern Europe, Central Europe and he was now entering Western Europe. He got his checklist out. He knew that something was coming up that he had to do. He looked down the list. "Number 7. Deliver presents. Well, I'm doing that now. Number 8. Return home. Well, I'm past the halfway point so I will be home shortly. Oh yes. Number 7b. I nearly forgot again. Collect Mrs Claus. I better remember to collect her. Otherwise, I'll be in big trouble with Mrs Claus when I do collect her, if I'm late. Skye is my next stop," said Santa.

Santa flew over to Skye and he landed on the roof of the thorN loPe. Mrs Claus was there waiting for him inside in the living room. She had packed everything that they needed to take back with them. "Oh, you made it back Mr Claus. I knew you would," said Mrs Claus, hugging and giving him a big kiss.

"Yes, I made it back safe and well," said Santa. Santa then started to explain all the things he had done, and seen and what the elves had done and what they had been doing at the North Pole in getting everything ready for Christmas.

Mrs Claus couldn't believe what she was hearing but she knew, deep down, that the elves would do what needed to be done for Christmas. They always did. Mrs Claus got all hers and Santa's stuff together. She was now ready to get into the sleigh with him. But how was she going to get in the sleigh? She couldn't climb up outside onto the roof. "How shall I get in the sleigh with you?" asked Mrs Claus.

"Don't you worry about that. Take my hand and I will take care of it," said Santa. Mrs Claus held onto Santa's hand. Santa rubbed his hat with his other hand, gave a nod of his head, stamped his left foot and, in the blink of an eye, they were both on the roof and in the sleigh.

"Wow! That was great," said Mrs Claus.

Santa just smiled. "What are we going to do about the thorN loPe? We can't just leave it how it is. It will be such a shame," said Mrs Claus.

"Don't you worry about that. I have two more deliveries to make here on Skye and everything will work out just right," said Santa.

Santa pulled on his reins. He knew where he needed to go first. He went to the estate agency to drop one of his letters off. Mrs Claus thought it may have been the keys to the cafe because the twelve-month lease was nearly finished. But she was wrong – she was, oh, so wrong! Santa then stopped at the last house on Skye. He went down and up the chimney so quick that, if you blinked, you would have missed it. "Are we done here, now, Mr Claus?" asked Mrs Claus.

"Yes, I think we are. Atlantic Ocean—here I come!" called out Santa.

Santa flew across the Atlantic Ocean. He finished delivering all the gifts and toys to the children of the world. He was done. He got his checklist out, just to double check that he had done everything. He checked it once. He checked it twice. Yes – finally everything was now completed. He could now do Number 8. Return home. "That's it, Mrs Claus. We can go home now. I'm all done," said Santa.

"That's good. I have enjoyed the sleigh ride with you tonight, Mr Claus, but I will be glad to get back home. I don't think I could do this every year with you," Mrs Claus said.

"I don't think we will have another year like this, Mrs Claus, and, if I do get any silly ideas again, please remind me of what I did this year—and stop me," said Santa.

Mrs Claus just smiled and held onto Mr Claus's arm.

They arrived back at the North Pole and all the elves were there, ready and waiting for them. You will never guess what Santa said to Blitzen as they returned to the North Pole. Go on, have a guess!

(No? Don't know? Well, Santa, as he does every year, says the same thing to Blitzen. I did mention it earlier in the story).

"Another white Christmas again this year!" Santa called out to Blitzen. Blitzen nodded in agreement with a reindeer smile on his snowy face. This year was even more special for them all because, during the year, they had thought that they would never hear those words again. The reindeers realised that sometimes the silliest things that are done are the things we love the most. That is why dads tell their dad-jokes. "Ha! Ha! Ha!" Sorry – I mean "Ho! Ho! Ho!"

They landed in the stable at the North Pole. The elves were super excited to see Mrs Claus – and Mrs Claus was just as excited to see them. There was a lot of clapping, dancing and cheering and, maybe, a few tears. But it was a wonderful time. "Only 364 days left till next Christmas Eve," called out Santa from his sleigh. Everyone laughed and cheered and all the elves started singing 'Jingle Bells'. "That's me all done for another year. I'm ready for bed now. I just want to thank all of you for doing what you have done this year. You carried on. You all still believed in the Christmas spirit. I lost mine along the way, for a short time, but, with you and the children of the world, I have now found it again," said Santa. Everyone cheered with excitement.

While Santa and Mrs Claus were fast asleep, the children of the world were enjoying all the toys and gifts Santa had delivered. Even though they hadn't got to see Santa this year, they were just so thankful that he had come and delivered everything that they wanted.

"This is El Leon, reporting on Christmas day. A Christmas miracle has occurred overnight. Even though he hasn't been seen or heard, Santa has come and delivered the presents. The children of the world are really happy," said El. Then, all of a sudden, out of nowhere, El shouted out live on TV. No one knows what made him do it but, from the top of his voice, he shouted, "I LOVE YOU SANTA!" The cameraman was shocked by what he had said, but El just grinned in acknowledgement. "Urm… urm… I don't know what made me say that, but it is true. Merry Christmas to you all!"

The camera then went off. The Christmas spirit of love, hope and believing was strong once again. People all over the world were remembering the true meaning of Christmas – to bring happiness to others, making up arguments, friends being friends, people repairing relationships, getting back together and to think of others. That is what Les Nit had done.

Christmas morning was here. Les Nit was just getting out of bed. He went into his mom and told her it was Christmas. They both got up and went downstairs and went to the Christmas tree. They sat on the floor and got their presents. There was one for Les and one for Les's mom. They weren't quite presents. They were more like letters. Les opened his first.

"Dear Les,

Where do I start? Thank-you for writing to me and still believing me in when others did not. I read your letter and you wanted no presents but only two wishes. I hope that I have done this for you and I wish you a Merry Christmas.

From Santa.

PS Take a look outside.

PPS Thank-you for the chat we had outside the thorN loPe.

It took Les a couple of seconds to take in what he had just read. "The chat?" he thought. "What chat? I spoke to the old man who runs the thorN loPe and nobody else." Then, it clicked. No wonder he had been so comfortable and happy around him. He was Santa. Les couldn't believe it.

Les got up and ran outside. He opened the door and there, outside waiting for him, was something he had always wanted – a brand new Mountain bike. It wasn't just any mountain bike but it was the Santa deluxe mountain bike. It was covered in

Christmas themed stickers, handlebars like antlers and lights like Rudolph's nose, shiny and bright. Les was happy. He was over the moon. He couldn't believe it.

Les went back inside and his mom was there sitting in silence, just holding up the letter she had just read. "Are you OK mom?" asked Les. His mom never said a word. She was in shock. Les took the letter and he started reading it.

"Ms Nit,

We are happy to let you know that you have won the thorN loPe Christmas competition. You have won the thorN loPe cafe on the island of Skye. The building is yours, complete with living quarters.

Merry Christmas, from the NP division.

Please contact the estate agent in the village for the completed paperwork.

PS – enclosed is the recipe to make the best hot chocolate that anybody has ever tasted. You will need this to keep the customers coming in.

Good Luck."

They were both in shock. Les asked his Mom, "Are you OK mom? Are you happy?"

Les's mom looked at him and said, "Yes, I am. Yes I am extremely happy. I have a new job. We have somewhere nice and new to live. Everything has turned out good for the both of us."

Les was so happy. He couldn't believe that his letter to Santa had worked and his Christmas wish had come true. His mom had a new job and, more importantly, she was happy. He did also get a cool brand new bike as well.

The following morning Santa got up. Again, he was awoken by Sualc. He was never woken up by Sualc on Boxing

Day. "Santa, you need to get up. Something has happened and you need to take a look quickly," said Sualc. Santa and Mrs Claus quickly got out of bed. Putting their dressing gowns on, they followed Sualc. Sualc was taking them to the Chimney room. "Santa, you need to take a look at something." Santa didn't know what was going on. He didn't know what to think. He opened the door.

As the door opened, he couldn't believe what he was seeing. Both Santa and Mrs Claus had their hands over their mouths. They were in shock. What was going on? This couldn't be happening. Santa stepped into the room. He had never seen it like this before – never. All around the room there were letters, more letters than you could imagine. The letters were coming down the chimney, quicker than a locomotive train. Santa had never seen this many letters a day after Christmas. Santa was so happy that the children of the world loved and appreciated everything he did but, also, that they appreciated what Mrs Claus, the reindeers and the elves do. They were a team and – what a team they make!

Santa picked up a letter and he started to read it.

"Babbo Natale,

Grazie per avermi portato tutti i miei giocattoli. Spero ti sia piaciuto il latte e il biscotto che ti ho lasciato. Buon Natale.

(Santa Claus, Thanks for bringing me all my toys. I hope you enjoyed the milk and biscuit I left you. Merry Christmas.

Gabriel, 8, Napoli."

Santa was relieved and he felt so happy. This is what he loved about Christmas and being Santa. The children of the world did need him and they did appreciate him. He just stood there in the chimney room smiling, watching all the letters come down the chimney. It was heart-warming for him. He loved being Santa and there would always be a Santa. He couldn't wait for the next 363 days to fly by so that he could deliver all the presents again. Santa decided he was going to have his favourite drink of hot chocolate, sit down and enjoy reading all the letters from the children and, probably, some adults' letters, as well. He was glad to be home but, more importantly, he was glad he was Santa again.

At the same time Santa as was reading his letters, Mr Sevle was opening up the estate agency. He opened the door and he picked up all the letters off the floor. He started to look through them. There was a letter with no stamp on it. It had been hand delivered. Mr Sevle decided to open this one first because it was hand delivered and with no stamp on it. "It must be important," he thought.

Mr Sevle began to read the letter.

"Dear Mr Sevle,

We have enjoyed our time on the island of Skye but me and Mary have decided it is now the right time for us to return home. We have enjoyed our twelve months here. We have made many new friends in the village, including your good self. The lease will be up next month so we will no longer be needing the lease of the thorN loPe. I hope you understand. In this case, however, I enclose the full asking price for the property because I wish to purchase it."

At this point Mr Sevle was a little confused. Why would you give up the lease and return home but then want to buy the property? It didn't make sense. Mr Sevle carried on reading. "You may find that this is a little bit strange and confusing that we want to purchase the property but we have decided that we would like to hand over the ownership of the thorN loPe to Ms Nit and Les Nit. We would be grateful if you would complete the necessary paperwork with them.

Thank you for all your help and we both wish you a very Merry Christmas.

Nick and Mary Claus."

Mr Sevle couldn't believe it. What a lovely gesture that they had made. How wonderful. It suddenly dawned on him when he saw the surname on the letter. It said "Claus." Could they have been Santa and Mrs Claus? They looked like them. It couldn't have been them, could it? Mr Sevle just smiled and carried on with his work.

The end.

CHARACTERS AND BUILDING NAMES

Les Nit: Read backwards it's Tinsel

Mr Sevle: Read backwards it's Elves

Sualc: Read backwards it's Claus

El Leon: Read backwards it's Noelle

Ego Orcs: Read backwards it's Scrooge

Flo Dur: Read backwards it's Rudolf

H C Nirg: Read backwards it's Grinch

Fle Sam X: Read backwards it's Xmas Elf

ThorN loPe: Is an anagram of North Pole. That is why the N and P are capitalised.

First Letter of each Chapter reads out: NO SANTA NO ELF

About the Author

This is my first ever story. Myself and my family love everything about Christmas and the joy and togetherness it brings. I am thirty-eight years old and have lived in West Bromwich all my life and have enjoyed reading stories to my three children. I have never thought about writing stories but now I have found this to be a passion I never knew I had. The memories we have made by reading will last with them for a long time and I hope that you can create memories with your children and family with my story. Please enjoy.